An Angel for Christmas

Spirit of the Christmas Star

E.F. Rose

An Angel for Christmas
Spirit of the Christmas Star

Written by E.F. Rose
www.facebook.com/DarkestRose13

ISBN: 979-8-9852112-7-6

Edited by: Kim Young of Kim's Fiction Proofreading & Editing Services

Warning:

Intended for mature audiences only (18+). This book contains a bit of naughty mixed in with the nice, light sexual content, and all of the Christmas feels.

If you wish upon a Christmas Star, and the Christmas spirit deems it special enough, it'll be granted...

Chapter 1

The Wish

Jackson watched his dad, Shane, hang the last ornament on the Christmas tree. A shiny, gold ball that contained his parents' names, a heart surrounding them. It was always the last one placed, as well as the first taken down after the new year.

It was also the only one that made his dad sad.

He didn't know exactly what happened to his father, just that when Jackson was two, he was taken away. His dad talked about him often, and always with a sad smile. Now, at the age of five, Jackson could clearly see the grief on his dad's face. He didn't really understand where it came from. All he knew was that he wanted to help him be happy.

And he desperately wanted his dad happy.

Sure, his dad wasn't always sad. He laughed and played with Jackson every chance he got, but the shadow was always there, lurking in the background. When his dad didn't think he was looking, it would descend over his face. Especially when they were around other couples.

Maybe that was why his dad was so sad. Maybe he was lonely.

With a small smile, Jackson nodded slightly. That was what he'd get his dad for Christmas. Someone to spend time with. But who? And how would he find them?

Jackson watched him touch the gold ornament before stepping back to look over the entire tree. The twinkling, white lights gave off a soft glow.

"Okay, kiddo. You ready for bed?"

His dad's voice drifted over to him, causing Jackson to blink a few times. "Yes."

"Why don't you start getting ready. I'll be right up to tuck you in."

With a smile, Jackson hopped off the couch and ran over to his dad, flinging his arms around his waist. The feeling of security in his dad's arms caused a warmth to spread through Jackson before he bounded up the stairs.

After brushing his teeth and putting on his pajamas, Jackson crawled into bed just as his dad walked through the door. "Story?"

"Of course," his dad said with a smile.

Stopping by the bookcase near the door, he picked out one of Jackson's new Christmas books. "Ready?"

Snuggling down into the covers, Jackson reached for his stuffed bear as his dad sat on the edge of his bed and opened the book.

Listening intently, Jackson couldn't help his giggles and gasps as his dad began to spin an incredible tale of hope, love, and Christmas magic. He had heard the story several times, but there was a particular part of the tale that really stood out to him this time. Grabbed his attention and became the only thing he could focus on.

"Daddy, is there really a Christmas Star?"

Pausing mid-sentence, his dad glanced down at him with a gentle smile. "There sure is. While you can always see it between December sixteenth through Christmas, it's brightest on December twenty-first."

Jackson looked at the calendar on his wall, eyes widening. "That's today."

"Yup. If there are no clouds, you'll be able to see it shining brighter than any of the other stars."

"Wow," Jackson breathed out, an idea quickly forming in his head. "If you make a wish on it, will it come true?"

"Well...," his dad started, then shrugged. "I guess anything is possible. After all, it is the season of miracles."

Jackson only half listened to the rest of the story. His mind remained stuck on the idea of wishing on the Christmas Star, and if that wish would really come true.

"And, thanks to that heartfelt wish, the family lived happily ever after."

Closing the book, his dad leaned over and kissed Jackson on the forehead. "Now, get some sleep."

Jackson watched his dad put the book away. "Night, Daddy."

"Night, Jackson. Love you." He turned off the light and pulled the door closed behind him, leaving it ajar.

Jackson lay on his side for a bit, staring out the window. Could a wish on the Christmas Star help his dad be happy?

Crawling out of bed, Jackson made his way over to the window, searching the sky. There! A brilliant, twinkling star, brighter than the ones around it. He took a deep breath.

"Hi. I'm Jackson. My daddy told me you could make wishes come true. Since it's almost Christmas, I hope that's true. You see, I was hoping you could help him. He's the best. He takes me to the park, makes me breakfast, gives the best hugs, reads to me every night. I love my dad so much. He makes me happy. I want him to be happy again, too." Sighing, he looked down at his hands. "I think he's lonely. He tries to hide it, but I can tell. I don't want him to be sad anymore. I wish… I wish for my dad to be happy. For him to smile all the time, even when nobody can see him."

Jackson stood there for a moment, gazing up at the bright star. Did he do it right? He'd never wished on a star before. It had to work. Like his dad said, it was Christmas. Anything was possible.

Jackson pulled his curtains closed and climbed back into bed. A smile on his face, he yanked his blanket up to his chin and snuggled his bear. He drifted off, excited to see what tomorrow would bring.

"Oh, that sweet child," Chiara breathed, gazing into one of her many mirrored snowflakes as she watched the young boy crawl back into his bed. While she was just one of many Christmas Spirits granting wishes of the deserving, Chiara specialized in the young.

Children were so special. While many wished for material things, like a puppy or new bike, some wanted more. They wished for something for their family, their friends, even people they didn't know. Those wishes were special.

Chiara smiled as the boy curled around an obviously well-loved teddy bear and closed his eyes. Humming softly, she turned to the book beside her. To an outsider, the pages looked blank. To her, Jackson's family's lives were spelled out. All their heartache, joy, hopes, dreams.

Shane had a sadness hanging over him. A hole in his heart after the loss of his husband. Yet there was so much love there, too. It was almost as if his very being reached out for another to share it with. How could she do anything but help fill that void? She knew he didn't need a replacement for the love he lost, knew he wouldn't accept that, but a new love. A different kind of love that would bring light and hope to the family.

A grin slowly formed on Chiara's lips. She knew just who to send.

She turned and reached into her pouch, grabbing a handful of stardust. Turning back to Jackson's snowflake, Chiara raised her fist and held it over the image of the sleeping boy.

"I have heard your wish, little one," she said softly. "Not only do I deem it special, I find it beautiful. May the light of the Christmas Star shine brightly upon you and yours this evening...and every evening to come."

She slowly relaxed her fist. Chiara watched the stardust float onto the snowflake, causing a silvery shimmer to encase it, becoming brighter and brighter.

Jackson and his dad were in for quite the surprise, and Chiara couldn't wait to watch it play out.

Chapter 2

The Loss

Shane rested his forehead against the doorframe as he listened to his little boy talk to the stars. Rubbing his chest, Shane felt a single tear run down his cheek. He thought he'd been able to hold it together, at least when around Jackson. Looked like his little boy had seen right through him.

On any other day of the year, he was usually able to mask the fact his heart was broken. But when the holidays rolled around, he just couldn't stop the pain from bleeding out.

David...

Just the thought caused his throat to tighten up and his very soul to cry out. Maybe if it had been a disease that had stolen his husband from him, it would be easier to deal with. But that wasn't the case.

That morning had started off just like any other. Waking up in each other's arms, Jackson bursting into the room and jumping onto the bed, demanding breakfast... Those last minutes together were all Shane could think about.

Maybe if he had fixed something besides eggs and toast, something that would have taken a little longer, David wouldn't have left for work when he did. Wouldn't have been on that bridge when it collapsed.

Blowing out an unsteady breath, Shane peeked into Jackson's room. In the light from the hallway, he could just make out his silhouette as he snuggled under the covers. That child was his world. After David was gone, he had dedicated all his time to making sure Jackson knew he was loved and felt safe.

Shane scrubbed his hand over his face as he walked down the hall to his own room. Jackson's soft words tore at him as he got ready for bed. The love and sweetness in his son almost broke him. But he knew if he gave in, he'd never be able to repair it.

Numb and mentally exhausted, he slid beneath the covers. His gaze locked onto the picture on his nightstand, just like every night. A smiling David stared back at him, arms wrapped around a sleeping baby swaddled in a blue blanket. The night they brought Jackson home from the hospital.

It had taken months to find a surrogate they liked and trusted, then several more to finalize everything. The biggest part of the journey had been waiting to hear the good news. When that day finally came, there were no words to describe how excited they were. But bringing Jackson home, holding him in their arms, felt even better.

They were complete, a family. Shane thought life would only continue to get better from there.

He was wrong. So very wrong.

"I miss you so much," he whispered, staring at the picture, eyes welling with tears.

When he'd gotten the call about the accident, his legs had given out, sending him crashing to the floor. Jackson had just turned two. They were planning on visiting Shane's brother the following weekend. Instead, he suddenly found himself arranging a funeral. It wasn't fair, and the pain from that day had never gone away.

David was the love of his life. There would never be another, and that thought seemed to hurt his soul even more than the memories.

Chapter 3

Breakfast And...

Waiting for the coffee to finish brewing, Shane leaned against the counter and stared at the Christmas tree in the living room. This had always been one of his favorite holidays. Seeing the smile on Jackson's face when he rushed into the room Christmas morning to see all the presents... It was one of the only things that made him smile after losing David.

Hearing the sound of running upstairs made Shane grin. Jackson was his whole world now. Nothing else mattered.

After what he overheard last night, Shane knew he needed to try harder to mask the pain he felt every day. No child deserved to be burdened with worry, especially when it came to a parent.

He turned toward the kitchen entrance just as Jackson came sprinting around the corner. His short, brown hair stuck up, his honey-brown eyes still slightly red from sleep.

"Morning, Daddy."

"Morning, buddy. Did you sleep good?"

"I did. I dreamt it was sunny and we were having a picnic."

"Yeah?" He opened his arms. The smiling boy ran at him. Grunting, as if his son had knocked the wind out of him, Shane lifted him up and carried him toward the kitchen table. Even at five years old, Jackson was a little small for his age. The doctors told him he may always be a little short. At only five-foot-five himself, Shane couldn't be upset about it. "You're getting so big. I think you might even be bigger than you were yesterday."

"You say that every morning, Daddy," Jackson giggled. "I'm no bigger."

"Are you sure?" Shane asked, setting Jackson onto a chair at the table. "I think you are. You've grown at least two feet since last night."

He laughed. "No. I still have the same two feet. See?" Sticking out his sock-clad feet, Jackson wiggled them around.

"So you do. Silly me." Shane ruffled his son's hair. "Now, what would you like for breakfast, young man?"

"Cheery-Oats!" Jackson belted out,

bouncing in his seat.

"You got it." Shane walked over to the cabinet and took out a bowl, then opened the fridge. "Water, juice, or milk?"

"Ooo... Juice. I love juice."

"Me, too."

Grabbing the milk and the orange juice, Shane turned back to the counter. Once he filled the bowl with cereal and milk, then poured a glass of juice, he set everything in front of Jackson.

"Here you go, kiddo."

"Thanks, Daddy," Jackson replied, already lifting a spoonful of cereal to his mouth.

Shane fixed himself a bowl and leaned back against the counter, watching his son for a few minutes. "So... What do you want to do today?"

Jackson shrugged, taking a big drink of juice. "Don't know. What about you?" He wiped the back of his hand across his mouth.

Shane also shrugged. "Don't know." He smirked as Jackson giggled.

"Daddy..."

Shane chuckled as he began to lift another

spoonful of cereal to his mouth, spoon pausing when he heard a loud thump out in front of the house.

"What was that?" Jackson asked, beginning to slide out of his seat.

Shane set his bowl on the counter. "Stop. Wait here. I'll go take a look."

Jackson pouted slightly as he settled back into the chair. Though he knew his son would only obey his order for as long as it took him to get to the front window, Shane took it as a small victory. In his haste to see what was going on outside before his son rushed up behind him, he misjudged the distance and smacked his forehead against the window.

"Shit," he cursed softly, rubbing his head.

"Oh... You said a bad word."

Shane spun around, seeing Jackson standing behind him. "No, I didn't." Before his son could say anything, Shane frowned. "And I thought I told you to wait at the table."

"I want to see."

"But I told you to–"

"Please, Daddy."

He sighed before turning back to the window. "What the..." Brows furrowed, Shane watched as a tall man slowly stood from the snow-covered ground. The man seemed slightly unsteady as he glanced around, absently wiping snow off his pants.

Feeling a light pressure on his hip, Shane glanced down to see Jackson wiggling between him and the window. “Who’s that?”

“I don’t know, buddy.” He looked back at the stranger standing on their lawn, long trench coat swaying slightly in the breeze.

Just as Shane was about to suggest they go back to the table to finish breakfast, the stranger turned their way, startling, green eyes locking with his brown ones. With a soft gasp, Shane took an involuntary step back, yet couldn’t look away.

The stranger’s shoulder-length, red hair curled at the ends, broad chest heaving as he released a puff of air, visible in the cold air. Between his chiseled features, muscular legs, full, kissable lips...

The man was the most handsome he had ever seen.

Shane’s stomach roiled and skin heated as the stranger’s eyes bored into his.

Something inside him wanted to open his front door, pull the man to him, and never let him go. And that scared the hell out of him.

Chapter 4

What The...?

Dax glanced around, confused. Where was he? What the hell just happened?

He groaned and slowly stood, wiping snow from his pants. Everywhere he looked, all he could see were maintained bushes and cookie-cutter homes. What the...

"Shit. I'm in freaking Small Town USA." Focusing on the decorations and several blowup Santas in the area, Dax let out a soft laugh. "And it's Christmas. Just...freaking...perfect."

It wasn't that he didn't like Christmas. He actually found this time of year to be one of the more endearing holidays the humans celebrated. He'd even been known to come down here to see what fun activities the humans were engaged in. He loved it all. From the decorations, to the games, to the myths associated with the holiday. The idea of a fat man using reindeer to fly from rooftop to rooftop to deliver gifts to children in one night was so fantastically incredible that Dax couldn't help but love it.

And he did love this time of year...if he were in the mood for it. Planned a visit. But as wetness seeped into his shoes and the cheery Santas towered over him, Dax just wanted to growl in frustration. He'd been unceremoniously yanked from his home after only getting the barest sip of his coffee in him.

Pulling his thoughts back to the matter at hand, Dax frowned as he once more looked at his surroundings. How did he get here? And why?

The last thing he remembered was sitting down to eat breakfast. He'd just taken a sip of coffee when he felt a pull in his chest. He remembered rubbing at it and frowning as he looked down. Then he was jerked right out the damn window! Didn't even have a chance to yell out or grab onto anything.

He quickly glanced over his shoulders and blew out a relieved breath, not seeing his wings. At least his magic was working. It would be hard enough to explain his sudden appearance, let alone having to justify the white wings sprouting from his back.

Shivering in the cold, Dax's fingers twitched. He felt a rush of power as his favorite trench coat settled over his shoulders.

"That's better," he murmured.

Well, whatever had brought him here would have to remain a mystery for now. He had a poker game scheduled in an hour. The guys would have a good laugh about this one.

Just as he was about to send himself home, Dax felt an overwhelming urge to look behind him. He focused on his surroundings, listened to his gut. It had never steered him wrong...

Turning slowly, Dax immediately met a human's gaze through the window of the house in front of him. And a very handsome human at that.

"Well, well, well..."

He watched the man step back. His eyes widened in surprise or fear, Dax couldn't tell which, yet were still warm and inviting.

"No sense in being rude. I should go introduce myself."

Smile on his face, Dax began to walk toward the front door. His mind reeled with what all this could mean. What the feelings swirling in his body could represent.

He'd heard about his friends finding their other halves, their soulmates, their amans, but had never really put a lot of stock into it. After all, he'd never found his.

But the stories he'd heard made him want to believe it was possible.

For the longest time, the idea there was someone out there for him was all he had thought about. But after more than two hundred years of searching, spending countless months hoping to find that special someone, to no avail, Dax had given up. Convinced himself that the stories he had heard were just that. Stories.

Now, when he'd finally gotten himself to where he was okay with being alone, here he was, standing in front of a house, filled with a warmth and peace he'd never experienced before.

Standing at the door, Dax slowly raised his hand and knocked. He heard several distinctive footsteps behind it, which surprised him. He was certain the only soul he'd sensed in the house was the man in the window. Then again, he'd been so shocked and focused on him that he may have been blind to anyone else. Opening his senses, he could indeed sense two souls. The gorgeous man and another, much younger soul.

A child.

He loved children.

Now, Dax was even more intrigued and eager to gain entry to the home.

He heard the footsteps of his amans get closer, his essence practically calling out to Dax as he finally came to a stop on the other side of the door. Dax could sense his nervousness, his unease...but the man's desire to meet him, be near him, was also there.

Not wanting to startle him, Dax took a step back and waited. He knew the man would open the door eventually.

After a moment, Dax heard the soft click of the deadbolt. Anticipation thrummed through him as he watched the door slowly begin to open.

Leaning a little to the side, Dax smiled as he came face to face with his amans. The man's eyes were still wide, the brown glinting in the early morning sun.

"Hello there," Dax said cheerfully.

"Um... Hello," he responded. "Can, um... Can I help you?"

"Oh, yes. Yes, you can." At the slight narrowing of the man's eyes, Dax amped up his smile. "I seem to have become lost. May I use your phone?"

"My phone? You don't have a cell phone?"

Cell phone. Right.

With his visits to Earth few and far between, Dax had forgotten how much things had changed over the last few decades. The may I use your phone excuse probably hadn't worked in a while.

"Yes… I mean, no. I don't have my cell phone. I… I lost it."

"So… You lost your cell phone, and now you're lost?"

"Yup."

"Well, um…"

"Oh, where are my manners? My name is Dax."

The man nodded slightly. "Shane. Where… Where did you come from?"

"My house," he responded, not wanting to lie.

"That's not–"

"So, about me borrowing your phone…"

Shane shook his head slightly. "If you wait here a moment, I'll grab my phone for you."

Even though it was pretty chilly outside, even for an angel, Dax physically felt Shane's unease. So not offering for him to wait inside was not only understandable, but happily excepted. Anything to make his amans feel more at ease.

The door had just barely closed when it eased back open again. Instead of seeing Shane, though, Dax's gaze fell on a young child. Brown eyes wide, the little boy stared up at him.

"Hello," Dax said, somewhat uneasy by the child's unwavering stare. Crouching down to the boy's level, he offered him a small smile. "My name is Dax."

The kid stared at him a moment longer before offering Dax a crooked smile. "I'm Jackson. What were you doing in the snow?"

Looking over his shoulder at the yard, then back at Jackson, he shrugged. "I fell."

"Did it hurt?"

"A bit, but I'm okay now."

"Okay."

"Okay," Dax nodded. He glanced over Jackson's shoulder. "Is your dad coming back?"

"He said he would."

Looking back at the boy, he saw Jackson still staring at him. "Is your mother home?"

Asking almost gutted Dax, but he wanted to know what he was dealing with. No matter how much his soul yearned for Shane, if his amans were already taken... Well, he would never break up a happy home. He'd leave, taking in the image of Shane to hold onto for eternity. Even though it would kill him.

"I don't have a mommy."

He barely managed to control the huge grin threatening to spread across his face. "No?"

"No, and my father left."

Dax frowned, confused. "He left?"

"Yeah, and Daddy's sad."

"Jackson, what did I say about opening the door to strangers?"

Dax looked over Jackson's shoulder, seeing Shane striding toward them. Giving Jackson a small smile, Dax stood again.

"I know, Daddy. But I wanted to see who it was."

"He was just letting me know you would be back soon."

"Yes, well..." Shane absently brushed some hair away from his son's forehead. "He still shouldn't open the door for a stranger."

"But he's not a stranger. He's Dax."

At Shane's scowl, Dax held up a hand. "We introduced ourselves." Glancing down at the boy, he nodded. "But your dad's right. You shouldn't open the door for strangers. Even though you know my name, I'm still a stranger."

As Jackson seemed to mull that over, Shane held out his cell phone.

Dax took it with a grateful smile. "Thank you. It will be just a moment." Taking a few steps away, painfully aware of Shane standing in his doorway, watching him, he frantically thought about who he could call.

A name suddenly popped into his head. One he hadn't thought about in some time. He hadn't talked to Grave since that night in Boca. And what a night it was. There had been too much alcohol, too much music, too much sex. By the time the sun rose, Dax had started searching for some aspirin, and Grave had been buried under a pile of sweaty bodies.

Won't he be surprised to hear from me, Dax thought with a mental laugh.

Shooting a quick smile at Shane over his shoulder, Dax quickly punched in his friend's number. Two rings later, he heard the familiar, gruff voice.

"Hello," he barked.

"Grave, it's Dax."

"No shit? It's been forever since you've been Earthside. What's going on?"

"Well..." He glanced around. "I'm not certain yet. I was just rudely pulled from my home and practically tossed here."

"And where is here?"

"Couldn't tell you. But I do have some interesting news."

"Yeah? And what's that? Did you finally realize living on Earth is way more fun that that stuffy realm you call home?"

"No... Well, yes, but probably not for the reasons you think." Dax frowned, knowing he wasn't explaining this right.

"Well, that's as clear as mud." He heard the laughter in Grave's voice. "Okay, I give. What's going on?"

"The area I landed in... My soulmate lives here. I just met him. In fact, I'm talking to you on his phone."

The silence on the other end was deafening. Glancing, over his shoulder, he spotted Shane crouched next to Jackson, both staring at him as they talked quietly. The morning sun shone down on them, giving them an almost ethereal glow. The depths he already cared for them both took his breath away. The stories he'd heard explained what would happen, but to actually go through it was completely unexpected.

"I'm sorry... You found your what?"

"My soulmate. My amans. I landed right in his front yard."

"You lucky bastard. I'm giving you a virtual slap on the back. But why are you calling me? If it were me, you can be sure the last thing I'd want to do is talk to your winged ass."

Dax snorted. "Trust me. This isn't what I wish I was doing right now. But I needed to come up with a story and told him I was lost. It was the first thing that came to mind when he demanded to know what I was doing in his yard."

Grave laughed loudly. "Please tell me how that conversation went."

"You mean after he looked at me like I was crazy?"

More laughter. Dax growled softly as he shifted and gave Shane a little wave, then turned back around.

"Are you finished?"

"Yes. Sorry," Grave said in between chuckles. "Only you, man. Anyway, tell me what I can do to help?"

"I don't want to freak him out and come on too strong. He's human, so I know he doesn't feel the pull the same way I do. But I also don't want to give him too much space. What should I do?"

"Well... You said you were lost, right?"

"Yeah."

"Okay. I'll pop over there in about a half hour and get you. That should give you enough time to start wooing him and–"

"Wooing?" Dax chuckled. "Who says that? I know I haven't been here in a while, but I'm pretty sure that word went out when–"

"Can I finish?"

Dax smiled. "Sorry. Sorry."

"Anyway," Grave said, sounding only slightly annoyed. "I'll get us a nearby place to stay. That way, you can be close, yet not smothering. Most humans don't like a person who hovers. Just tell him you're visiting somebody in town, and that's why your dumb ass got lost."

"Thanks," Dax mumbled. "I think that may work."

"Dax?"

He spun, seeing both Shane and Jackson standing mere feet behind him.

"Is everything okay?"

"Oh, yeah. I was..."

"Tell him you're trying to figure out where you are so you can give me directions," Grave directed.

Of course he'd heard. He and Dax were the same in many respects. Angel or demon... It didn't matter. They both had strong powers, and enhanced hearing was only one of them.

"I was just trying to figure out where I am so I can have my friend come pick me up."

"Oh." He frowned slightly. At least it looked like a frown. It was there and gone so quickly, Dax couldn't be sure. However, all he saw now was the soft smile that graced Shane's face. "Is he familiar with Morton?" With a quick yes from Grave on the other end of the phone, Dax nodded. "Okay. If he goes north down Alburne and turns right on Deep Ridge, we're the fifth house on the right." He nodded at the car in the driveway. "Bright blue Toyota out front. He can't miss it."

After repeating the instructions to Grave, Dax smiled and hung up, handing the phone back to Shane. "Thank you."

"Of course," Shane murmured. "Your friend is coming to get you?"

"Yeah. I'm actually here on vacation. I decided to explore a bit and got turned around.

Truthfully…" Dax chuckled. "I'm not even sure how I ended up here."

"That's crazy."

"Yeah."

"Well…" Shane cleared his throat. "It's pretty cold out here. Would you like to wait inside?"

Gazing into Shane's eyes, Dax felt warmth building within him. His amans was worried he was cold! It was such a little thing, but as new as these feelings were, it was everything.

"I'd love to."

"We have hot chocolate."

Glancing down at Jackson, he couldn't help the smile that spread across his face. "Fantastic. I love hot chocolate."

Following Shane and his little boy into the house, Dax took a deep breath. This was a start. He had his foot in the door…literally.

Now he just had to figure out how to go about wooing him.

Chapter 5

This Is Not A Date

"Daddy, when is Dax coming back?"

Glancing over at Jackson, Shane smiled. His son was fascinated with Dax. It was both adorable and troublesome how quickly the man had gone from stranger to friend.

After getting everyone in from the cold yesterday, Shane had made some coffee and hot cocoa, then they'd all sat around the kitchen table, talking, laughing, enjoying their drinks.

That half hour had made him feel the calmest he'd felt in a while. He couldn't remember the last time he'd smiled or laughed so much. And the look of joy on Jackson's face had been wonderful, especially after the wish his little man had made the previous night.

There was just something about Dax that... He couldn't describe it. Almost called to him. That made him want to latch onto the man and never let go. But that was crazy. Shane hardly knew the guy. Hell, it had taken David almost four months to wear Shane down and get him to go out with him. Another two years before he said yes to being engaged. One-and-a-half years before they got married. Shane had always taken relationships slowly. So wanting to jump into something with Dax was so out of the norm that he should probably be more concerned than he was.

Since opening the front door, though, Shane had been filled with so many questions, so many feelings that he couldn't explain. But nothing had stopped him from agreeing to show Dax around Morton.

He wasn't even sure how that happened. They'd started talking about the places they'd both been. The next thing he knew, Dax asked if he'd show him around town. And he'd immediately said yes.

It wasn't until Dax's friend had picked him up and he'd watched the car disappear around the corner that he realized what he'd just agreed to. Which was quickly followed by wondering who he could get to watch Jackson on such short notice.

Wracking his brain, a name popped up. Cassie, his best friend. He called, letting her know what was going on. Luckily for Shane, she was more than happy to watch him for a few hours, telling him she'd pick Jackson up and bring him back to her house “just in case”.

Shane argued that it was not a date. But all Cassie did was laugh and tell him when to have Jackson ready, hanging up before Shane could respond.

“I’m going to see Dax today, remember? That’s why you’re going over to Cassie’s to watch a movie.”

“But, Daddy,” Jackson pouted, “I want to hang out with Dax, too.”

“Maybe another day, kiddo. You get to hang out with Cassie today. You like her, don’t you?”

“Yes.”

“Then you’ll have a good time. I’ll ask Dax how long he’s going to be here. Maybe we can figure out a time for all of us to get together before he leaves.”

“I don’t want him to leave,” Jackson whined.

Neither do I, Shane thought.

“Why don’t you head upstairs and get ready? Cassie should be here in just a few.”

Jackson sighed. “Okay…”

Listening to his son run up the stairs,

Shane rolled his eyes. “No running!”

“Okay,” Jackson yelled, slowing to a fast walk.

Shane took another sip of coffee and looked at the time display on the oven. Almost 11:30. Dax would arrive at 11:45. Shane figured they’d head out to lunch at one of his favorite restaurants, then walk through downtown to see all the shops decorated for Christmas. Morton wasn’t very big, only a little under fifteen thousand people called this town home, but its downtown was a sight to see. Especially during the holidays, the focal point a 30-foot-tall, beautifully decorated tree.

Hearing a knock, Shane walked to the door, opening it.

“Hey, love.” Cassie smiled, going in for a quick hug and kiss on the cheek before walking into the house. “Is the little man ready yet?”

“He’ll be down in a few minutes.”

“Good.” She waggled her brows. “And when is your date showing up?”

Shane groaned. “It’s not a date, Cassie, and Dax should be here in about fifteen minutes.”

She rolled her eyes and walked to the stairs. “You ready, munchkin?!” she yelled. “It’s your favorite aunt!"

"You're his only aunt," Shane mumbled, quietly laughing as she flipped him off behind her back.

"Aunt Cassie!" Jackson squealed, running toward the stairs.

Shane strode to the stairs. "You'd better not be running. You know what we talked about."

"I'm not, Daddy."

Shane watched as Jackson slowly made his way down the stairs, holding onto the railing with one hand, his other gripping the strap of his backpack.

"Here I am," he exclaimed, jumping off the last step.

"There you are." Cassie engulfed him in a huge hug. "Are you ready? We need to get out of here before your daddy's date shows up." She winked at Shane.

Jackson's brows furrowed as he looked at his dad, then back at Cassie. "What's a date?"

"A date is when two people go out to spend time together. Like going to eat or see a movie."

Shane glared at Cassie as Jackson started

giggling. “So Daddy has a play date?”

“That’s right,” Cassie said, huge smile on her face. “Your Daddy and Dax have a play date today. So we’re going to hang out while they spend some time together.”

“Why can’t we go?”

“Yeah, Shane.” She laughed. “Why can’t we go, too?”

Sending one last glare her way, Shane glanced down at his son. “I’m just going to show Dax around town. You’d be bored, so I thought you would have more fun hanging out with Cassie.”

Jackson’s face fell. “Oh.”

“But remember…” Shane pulled him in for hug. “I promised I’d talk to Dax and see if we can all get together before he leaves.”

“Okay,” Jackson uttered, voice muffled against Shane’s stomach.

“Okay.” Shane leaned down and kissed the top of his head. “Let’s get you all bundled up so you and Cassie can go. You guys have a movie to watch.”

“And popcorn to eat,” Cassie piped up. “I also may or may not have made some Christmas cookies.”

At that, Jackson perked up. "Yay! Cookies."

"Yay," Cassie laughed.

It took them about five minutes to wrestle Jackson into his winter coat and snow boots. Shane checked through his backpack, making sure he had everything he needed. After adding a blanket and a few snack bars, Shane zipped it up and they walked out into the cold.

"Let's get you buckled up." Helping Jackson into the car, Shane leaned in to fasten his seat belt.

After getting a promise that he'd behave himself, Shane kissed the top of Jackson's head and closed the door.

Cassie gave Shane a quick hug, then walked around the front of the car and opened her door. "Just give me a call when you get back and I'll bring him home."

"Will do. Thanks again for watching him for me."

"You know I'd never turn down a chance to spend time with Jackson." She smiled as she leaned on the top of the car, lowering her voice. "You have fun on your date. I expect to hear all the hot and sexy details."

"It's not a date," Shane insisted.

"You can call it whatever you want. But..." Cassie gave him a lude wink, "deep down, you know the truth. Have fun."

Shane watched Cassie pull away, Jackson spinning in his seat and excitedly waving over his shoulder. He released a long sigh as he waved back.

This wasn't a date. It was just a guy taking a new friend out for lunch and a tour of the town. Nothing more, nothing less.

He repeated that over and over in his head as he saw a car drive around the corner and pull up to the curb. The blue BMW glittered in the sun, though it didn't outshine Dax's smile or the twinkle in his eyes.

Who was he kidding? While this may not be a date, he definitely wished it were.

Chapter 6

This Is Definitely A Date

Dax's eyes stayed on Shane's as he got out of Grave's car and made his way up the driveway.

Before he left, Grave had reminded him to take it slow. He needed to remember that Shane was a human and would not react to the situation the same way he would.

If Shane were a paranormal, they would already be together. Their eyes would have met, they would have recognized the pull, and that would have been that. Sure, there was no guarantee everything would be sunshine and rainbows. Every relationship, human or paranormal, required work. But with that added pull in place, that overwhelming urge to be with each other, it would work out.

But with Shane being a human, it was going to take a lot more work to get their relationship going.

Once it did, he was going to have to

introduce Shane to a whole new world. One that he had no idea existed. It would be a long conversation filled with questions, confusion. And Dax had no idea how to go about starting it.

Grave offered to, quite literally, pop in once he started the discussion. But Dax wasn't sure how Shane would handle seeing somebody else suddenly in the room. He'd told Grave as much, at which time the demon had just shrugged and gave him a sinister smile. The same one that made others shiver and back away slowly. But Dax had just rolled his eyes.

Looking at Shanc, Dax felt his heart rate increase. Now he was going to have someone by his side. Someone he could count on, confide in.

"Hey," Dax said easily.

"Hi," Shane responded, a slight blush covering his cheeks. "My friend, Cassie, just picked up Jackson. Would you like to come in while I grab everything and lock up?"

"Sure. Was your friend okay with watching him?"

"Absolutely." Shane smiled as they walked back to the house. "They love spending time together."

Dax followed him into the house and stood in the doorway as Shane grabbed his phone and keys off the kitchen counter. "So, what do you have planned for us today?"

"Well, I was thinking we would get a little bite to eat, then walk around downtown. They always decorate it beautifully this time of year."

"Sounds nice."

As Shane shrugged into a coat, Dax couldn't help but admire the play of muscles beneath the man's shirt. Shane was by no means a muscular man, but he had enough that it showed he took care of himself.

"Ready?" Shane asked, looking up at him.

Dax swallowed hard, trying to get the mental picture of a shirtless Shane out of his head. "Whenever you are. Since I'm parked in the driveway, how about I drive?"

Shane contemplated a moment, then nodded. They were soon on the road, the conversation flowing easily.

Pulling into a parking spot in front of a cute restaurant, Dax looked around with appreciation. "Wow. The town really goes all out with the decorations."

"We do love our **holidays**." Shane opened the door and got out of the car. Dax followed, staring at his amans over the roof of the vehicle as the man continued to look around them. "Whether it be Christmas, Fourth of July,

Halloween... It doesn't matter. Anything you can decorate for, we do it. I've always loved it."

"It looks amazing. I love Christmas. It's always been one of my favorite holidays. I periodically come down here to look at all the decorations."

Realizing what he had said, Dax sucked in a quick breath as he made his way over to where Shane stood, hoping he didn't pick up on it, silently reminding himself to watch his words. At least for now.

Shane's expression fell for a second before it brightened again and he smiled. "It's one of my favorites, too."

"Yet it also makes you sad." Dax hadn't planned on pointing it out, but he just couldn't help it. He could practically feel the pain radiating off him.

Shane just amped up his smile. "Holidays are sometimes an emotional time for people.

"So, you hungry?"

Deciding not to comment on the change of subject, figuring Shane would share when he was ready, Dax nodded. They entered the small restaurant, the smell of baked goods and fresh coffee reaching his nose. Taking a deep breath, he let the magic of the holiday season fill him. His own magic reacted strongly to the joy and love that seemed to infuse the interior. Dax had to physically concentrate to keep it from getting out of control; otherwise, he ran the risk of shaking the pictures off the walls, the tables flipping, the lights bulbs and windows exploding. It had been a long time since his magic had gotten away from him, but there was always something about being around such an emotionally charged group of people that brought him to the edge. People filled with joy and love. But that was the wonder of this season. One of the many reasons he loved coming down here during this time.

Dax had figured the place would be busy with the lunch crowd, but he was pleasantly surprised to see very few tables occupied. Which was nice, considering his stomach chose that moment to announce the fact that he was starving.

Shane chuckled softly as a waitress beckoned them toward a booth, placing menus in front of them and telling them she'd be right back to take their order. Glancing at the menu, Dax's eyes immediately went to a picture of golden-brown French toast, mouth instantly watering.

"Do you know what you want?" he asked, placing his menu back onto the table.

Shane glanced at him over the top of the menu, eyes sparkling with laughter. "You'd think I would, seeing how often I come here." His gaze dipped back down to the menu. "I can just never seem to decide. Everything here is wonderful."

Dax just sat there, smiling as he listened to Shane mutter to himself about what he was in the mood for. By the time the waitress walked up, offering them coffee, they had both decided.

"So, do you travel a lot?"

Shane's question as the waitress walked away was expected, given the few bits Dax had mentioned about himself. "Um..." Not wanting to lie, he decided to get as close to the truth as he could without revealing anything. "I do, actually."

"Oh? For work?"

"Mostly, though I do like to just visit places."

"I've always wanted to travel."

At the wistfulness in his voice, Dax instinctively reached out and placed his hand on Shane's. "It's never too late to see what wonders exist outside your home."

"Maybe... With Jackson so young, though, it'll probably be a few years before I even consider going on any type of vacation." Shane gave Dax a smile that took his breath away. "When he's older and can appreciate it more, I'll take him somewhere spectacular."

"That sounds amazing."

Dax glanced down at his hand still on Shane's, thumb moving slightly. The feeling of his skin beneath his fingers caused a warmth to spread through him. He felt Shane tense slightly before pulling away and placing his hands in his lap, giving him a sheepish grin. Dax just smiled.

"So, um... What do you do for work?"

It took Dax a minute to process the question. "I... I work with a group that helps people in need."

"Like a non-profit?"

"Kind of."

Thankfully, the waitress chose that moment to walk up with their food, telling them to let her know if they needed anything else. After pouring syrup all over his French toast, Dax took a big bite, humming appreciatively. The minute the syrupy, buttery goodness hit his tongue, he lost himself in the flavor. Quickly taking another bite, Dax groaned. He licked some syrup off of his lips and glanced up, seeing Shane staring at him, smirking.

"What?" he asked around his mouthful of food.

"The noises you're making..." Shane chuckled. "That must be some good French toast. The most amazing French toast ever."

Feeling his cheeks warm, Dax swallowed his bite. "Yes, well... It's been a while since I've had this." He eyed the turkey club and fries in front of Shane. "Aren't you hungry?"

"Famished, actually. I was just caught up in your..." Shane waved his hand through the air, "enthusiasm. It's very distracting."

"Sorry," Dax said, smiling as he took another big bite, followed by a large piece of bacon.

Shane laughed. "No, you're not." He popped a few fries into his mouth. "But that's okay. It's good to show your appreciation when you like something."

Dax gazed into his eyes. "Oh, I definitely have no problem showing my appreciation for something I like."

Shane suddenly looked flustered, mouth opening and closing as he seemed to battle with himself on how to respond. Raising an eyebrow, Dax silently nodded for him to say whatever was on his mind.

"I'm so out of practice with this," Shane muttered, taking a sip of water. His confidence from moments ago seemed to melt away, replaced with vulnerability.

"This?"

"Flirting," he blurted. "I lost my husband a few years ago. Since then, I've made Jackson my entire focus. I haven't even wanted to talk to anyone, let alone flirt with them."

"Understandable."

"So I just feel like I'm out of my comfort zone here."

"I think you're doing great."

"Thanks," he sighed and looked down, seeming to concentrate on his sandwich.

Deciding to give his amans a few minutes to gather himself, Dax finished his French toast and sat back, sipping his cup of coffee. Shane seemed to be purposely not looking his way as he ate, which he found extremely endearing. He was a good-looking man, but this sudden shyness pulled at Dax's heart. The more he learned about Shane, the more he observed him, the greater his feelings became.

It was like he had been drowning, merely existing before he landed in the snow.

Shane was quickly becoming as important to him as the very air he breathed. And he couldn't wait until he could start showing it.

"Are you gentleman all done here?"

Glancing at Shane's now empty plate, Dax smiled up at the waitress. "I believe we are."

"Fantastic. I'll just leave this here." The woman set their check onto the table and grabbed their plates. "There's no rush. You two have a Merry Christmas."

"Thank you. You, too," they both said as she turned and walked away.

Dax grabbed the check before Shane could, earning him a scowl. He grinned at his amans as he left a generous tip on the table and slid out of the booth.

"How was everything?" the smiling girl at the counter asked, taking the check and money from Dax.

“It was really good.”

“Wonderful to hear.”

Shelly, according to her name tag, hummed as she made quick work of ringing them up. Thank goodness Grave had reminded him to think up some cash. Not usually needing it, he’d have completely forgotten, and this date would have definitely taken a different turn. Sure, Shane acted a little angry that he wasn’t allowed to pay for his meal, but Dax knew better. If this was to be considered a date, he didn’t want to stick Shane with the bill. How sad would that have been.

“Here ya go,” Shelly said cheerfully, breaking into his thoughts. He reached out for his change. “Y’all enjoy the rest of your day and have a Merry Christmas.”

“Thank you. Merry Christmas to you, too.”

Dax pulled the door open, motioning for Shane to walk through first.

“Thank you for lunch,” Shane said as he passed.

“You’re very welcome.”

They walked in comfortable silence as they passed one quaint store after another. Each had a decorated window...wreaths, ornaments, Santas, fake snow, Christmas villages. Everything about this town was cheerful, endearing. Between the decorations and the soft snow crunching beneath their feet, this was exactly the type of place that came to mind when he thought of the holidays. Dax loved everything about it. The allure made better by the man at his side.

Shane pointed out the major attractions. From the town library, which had been built in the early eighteen hundreds, to the bakery, which had been owned by the same family since the early sixties, to the town hall, wreaths hanging on the heavy, hand-hewn, oak doors. He delivered each story with a reverence that only came from someone who had grown up around the history.

Once they reached the end of the street, Shane paused. Dax looked on in wonder at the gorgeous, vine-covered entrance to a beautiful garden. From what he could see just beyond the gate, a stone path, which had been cleared of snow, wound through the grounds, Christmas lights covering bushes lining either side. It looked...magical, ethereal.

"That's our town's garden. During the spring and summer, it's filled with different flowers. With all the various colors and scents, it's beautiful. During winter, the town decorates it like our own little winter wonderland. Jackson loves walking through it. I thought…" He swallowed hard. "Well, I was wondering if you would like to check it out?"

The slight blush was back on Shane's face. While he could say it was from the cool air, Dax knew better. He felt the need, the want, as well as the uncertainty swirling around him.

Reaching down, hoping to dispel his insecurity, he took Shane's hand and gave it a gentle squeeze, smiling. "There's nowhere else I'd rather be."

The blush seemed to intensify as Shane gave him a slight nod before they began walking toward the garden's entrance. It wasn't until they passed under the enchanting archway that Dax realized Shane had yet to release his hand. Actually, it felt like the man held on tighter with each step. Like he didn't want to let go.

A feeling Dax recognized echoing within himself.

Chapter 7

I Want You To Be My Future...

Shane reveled in the feeling of Dax's skin against his. It had been so long since he'd enjoyed something as simple as holding someone's hand.

As they walked through the garden, he sighed in contentment. It truly was beautiful. Twinkling lights in the bushes, snow covering everything. And with the winter clouds, there was just enough soft light to make the snow sparkle, like thousands of diamonds littered the ground. It was all quite romantic.

For a moment, Shane worried it was too romantic. While he tried to convince himself this was not a date, a little voice in his head kept telling him to quit fooling himself. Even worse, this was his idea. So, really, he was the one to blame here. But was that such a bad thing? Would being on a date with Dax be so terrible?

He didn't know why he fought his feelings. He'd never felt so comfortable with someone, so relaxed. Not even David, which might be why he was so on the fence.

Shane took a deep breath, smelling something he'd come to associate with Dax. A mixture of cinnamon and toasted marshmallow. He couldn't stop a soft groan from escaping as he took another deep breath.

"Shane?"

He blinked a few times before glancing up. "Hmm?"

The laughter in Dax's eyes told him he'd been caught. "I asked how long this garden has been here."

"Oh, um... It's been around since shortly after the town was founded. Right around the same time as the library was finished. The story is the first man who settled here had a wife who loved gardens. So he had this made for her. That's why the locals call it Emma's Garden, even though the official name is The Garden."

Dax smiled, looking around. "Well, it's gorgeous. I can see why the town has kept it up all of this time."

"The Garden is the pride and joy of our little town."

Shane stopped. They'd made it to the center, where the walkway circled a bronze statue of a beautiful woman, hands clasped before her, billowing robes flowing to her feet. Shane focused on her face. Eyes gazing out over the landscape, head slightly tilted. She held a sense of serenity about her. Though everyone had a theory, he'd never heard a solid story of who she was. Hell, nobody even knew who made it. The only clue they had were the initials G.R. on her base.

All Shane knew was he'd always felt a calmness surround him when in her presence.

Turning his head, he watched Dax's expression as he marveled at the statue.

"She's beautiful," he murmured, releasing Shane's hand and stepping closer. He reached out, as if to touch her, then clenched his hand and lowered it back to his side.

"She really is. And she's been here a long time, watching over The Garden. Some would argue she's also watching over the town."

"Well, she's stunning. The detail, even after all this time, is perfect."

Dax stepped back and grasped Shane's hand once again, as if it were the most natural thing in the world. They stood there, looking at the snow-covered statue, the soft twinkling of the lights on the bushes giving the area a delicate glow.

"Thank you."

At the soft words, Shane looked up at Dax. His red hair swayed slightly in the breeze, eyes gazing into Shane's. "For what?"

"For showing me around. For taking time out of your day. For just being you."

"For being me?"

Dax stepped closer. "Yes," he murmured. "You have no idea how special you are."

He searched Dax's eyes. His breath caught at the want and need he saw. The same feelings that seemed to echo his own. Licking his lips, he watched Dax's gaze drop, eyes darkening.

Taking a chance, Shane closed his eyes and leaned up, his lips connecting with Dax's. Their kiss was hesitant at first, testing the other, making sure this was okay.

He was definitely okay with this. He'd wanted to kiss this man the second he saw him standing in his yard.

With a moan, Dax's arms went around him, yanking him flush against him as he deepened the kiss.

Shifting slightly, Shane felt Dax's hardness rub against him, making a tingle travel up his spine. It had been too long since he'd been with somebody. Because of that, the need to lose himself in this moment almost overwhelmed him.

Not even the cold wind or snow that had started to fall could douse the flames flaring inside him. But he knew they couldn't stay out here forever. The chill would soon become a problem.

And he knew just how to get warm. Shane's thoughts ran rampant with images of them in bed, tangled in the sheets.

Hoping Dax was on the same page...and, judging by the feeling of him, he was...Shane slowly stepped away from the hard, warm body.

"Shane?" Dax panted, confusion covering his face.

"It's starting to snow," Shane responded, taking hold of Dax's hand. "We should get someplace warm."

"Someplace warm?"

"I thought we could head back to my place."

"Your place?"

Shane smiled slyly as he pulled Dax down the path and toward the entrance. By the time they made it back to Dax's car, the wind had picked up, snow increasing.

Shane slipped into the passenger seat as Dax quickly moved around the front of the car, practically diving behind the wheel.

"Wow. The storm is really building," Dax said. Hitting the ignition button, then the seat warmers, they soon began to thaw out, making them both sigh in contentment.

Sinking back into the cream-colored leather, Shane fastened his seat belt before giving Dax a soft smile. "So…"

"So…" Dax leaned over and nipped Shane's bottom lip. "Your place?"

He opened his mouth to say yes, then paused. Was he ready for this? He didn't know much about Dax. Now that the adrenaline from their kiss had started to fade, he couldn't help but wonder if he were jumping into this too quickly. He wasn't that type of person. Never had been. Always weighed all his options first.

Yet something about Dax was different. Shane felt happier than he had in a long time. Even thinking about David was manageable now, unlike the soul-crushing agony his name would have brought on only a few days ago.

That had to mean something.

"Nothing needs to happen once we get to your house, Shane. We can just take time to get to know one another."

Dax's deep voice brought Shane out of his musings. Looking at the man next to him, he realized that, while he many not know him in the normal sense, his soul knew him, yearned for him. Plus, everything Dax had done and said up until that point spoke volumes. Showed him this man was a good person. He was caring, funny, truly seemed to enjoy Shane's company. Then there was the way he'd been with Jackson. Laughing at his son's jokes, answering questions, listening attentively.

That was really all Shane needed to know.

"Let's head back to my house," he said with a smile, leaning over to place a chaste kiss on Dax's lips. "Then we'll see where the afternoon takes us."

"Sounds good to me."

Giving him one last kiss, Dax straightened and fastened his own seat belt before pulling away from the curb, joining the slowly moving cars headed through town.

As Dax pulled off the main road and onto the back street, Shane felt the car slide slightly in the snow. He usually found this short drive to be beautiful. The houses becoming farther apart, wooded areas lining the roads... Today, though, with the wind blowing and snow falling heavily, all he felt was anxiety.

Gripping the door handle, Shane forced out a breath he hadn't realized he'd been holding. "This sure came out of nowhere."

"Yeah, and it doesn't seem to be letting up. We're almost there, though."

Dax gripped the wheel, knuckles whitening. Regardless of how calm he appeared, Shane saw the tension in his body, in the lines of his face.

"No matter how many storms I've been through, I'll never get used to them," Shane uttered.

"I'm sure, but like I said, we're almost back. Just a few more turns and–"

The car shuddered and swerved to the left, the wind slamming into them. As Dax fought to regain control, Shane's eyes widened at what he saw out the windshield.

Whether from the weight of the snow or the strength of the wind, a massive tree limb broke free and fell toward the road. There was no stopping it, no way to avoid it.

"Dax! Look out!"

Bracing himself, Shane was only partially aware of Dax grabbing his arm and yelling for him to hold on. The air around him seem to electrify, almost like static, the tree heading toward the car.

Shane's thoughts went to Jackson. If he didn't make it out of this, and the chances of that were fairly good, he knew Cassie would take care of him. But it hurt to think he wouldn't be there to see him grow up, be there when he graduated from high school, be at his wedding, see him become the man Shane knew he would be.

"No!" he screamed.

He turned his head, eyes closed against the inevitable. Even so, he could see a glow fill the car, growing brighter with each second, heat washing over him. Glass shattered. Metal groaned. Then he knew nothing but darkness.

Chapter 8

This Is Not The End

As soon as Dax saw the limb break free, realizing it was going to be a direct hit, he knew he could only do one thing. Yelling for him to hold on, he grabbed onto Shane's arm with one hand, bracing himself against the dash with the other. With barely a thought, his power began to build, sparking against his skin.

Once he felt his power reach its peak, Dax released his hold on the dash and gripped Shane's arm tighter just as the tree hit in a cacophony of grinding metal and shattering glass.

His energy burst from him, encircling them with swirling lightning and mist, quickly moving them to the safety of the side of the road.

He gently lay a now unconscious Shane on the ground, then looked at the car, chest heaving. The front half of it, including the driver and passenger seats, were now nothing but flattened metal, the massive limb lying across it.

Hearing Shane groan, Dax knew he needed to get him back to his house, the snow still coming down in buckets, the wind whipping around them.

"Come, my amans. Let's get you home," Dax whispered, scooping Shane up into his arms. Glancing around to make sure they were alone, he released his wings in a flash of light. They slid seamlessly through the almost invisible slits in his shirt and coat. All angels had them. Saved time and money on either repairing your clothes or buying new.

The tips of his white feathers just brushed the ground as he stood, Shane cradled against his chest. Dax spread his wings and ruffled them slightly, smiling. The feeling was amazing. Almost like denying yourself something for years, then being able to experience it again. Giving them one last shake, he looked up and, with one good flap, launched them into the air.

He hoped he was able to get Shane home before he fully regained consciousness. That way, he could ease him into the conversation he knew was probably coming. Dax wracked his brain, trying to come up with a good answer to the fact they got out of the car without a scratch.

Unfortunately, luck was not on his side this time.

"What the fuck?!" Shane screeched, tensing, arms wrapping around Dax's neck like a vice.

"It's okay. I've got you."

"You... We're flying, Dax. Flying! How..." His shrill voice cracked as he looked one way, then another.

"We're almost to your house, Sha–"

"Oh, my god! You have... You have wings!"

Dax glanced at Shane's wide-eyed stare. "Yes, I do." When he opened his mouth again, Dax continued. "I'll explain everything when we get to your house. I promise."

"O-okay...," Shane responded, voice wobbling, grip still tight around Dax's neck.

Gliding along with the wind, Dax made his way toward Shane's house. Quickly glancing around, he blew out a small breath when he didn't see anybody. Probably hiding out from the storm. The less chance he had of being noticed, the better. Not that it hadn't happened before. It was just such a hassle. Wiping someone's memory of the encounter was always so taxing.

Landing in the back yard, he set Shane on the ground, keeping hold of him until he has his footing. Spreading his wings, he shielded them as they walked to the door, Shane opening it. Dax took a second to shake the snow off his wings and gather his thoughts before walking into the house, having to duck through the doorway.

Shane shrugged off his coat and threw it across the kitchen table, then sat, running a hand through his damp hair. Spinning in the chair, he quickly grabbed a bottle of rum and a glass from the curio cabinet, pouring himself a healthy amount and downing it.

That's not good, Dax thought.

Shane winced at the burn as it slid down his throat, then glanced up at Dax. "Okay... Please tell me this is a dream. That we didn't just escape an accident without a scratch. That we didn't fly here. That you don't have wings."

"Well..." Not knowing what to say, he just stood by the table, shifting from foot to foot.

Shane gestured to a chair. "You should probably sit..." Then he furrowed his brows, glancing over Dax's shoulder. "Can you sit with those?"

"Oh, yes. Just a minute." Dax grinned slightly, his wings retracting. Taking off his coat and hanging it on the back of the chair, he sat. "So..." He blew out a breath. "Honestly, I don't even know where to start."

"How about this... Who are you? Where did you come from?"

Meeting Shane's gaze, Dax reached for the glass and bottle. He poured a small amount before pushing the glass toward Shane, recapping the bottle. "Do you want me to ease you into everything? Or just tell you?"

"Just..." He swallowed. "Just tell me."

"Okay." Dax rested his arms on the table. "I'm an angel. I come from a place the paranormal world calls the Angelic Realm. I got us out of that car using my energy...white light...power." He shrugged. "Whatever you want to call it.

"But I also need you to understand something. Something I felt the second I saw you. I really like you, Shane. Your soul calls to me. You are my soulmate, what we call amans, and if you'll let me, I will spend the rest of eternity making you happy."

"Wow...," Shane breathed, then shook his head. "That is a lot to take in at one time. Let's dissect it all."

"Absolutely." Dax nodded. "Where do you want to start?"

"How about with you being an angel?"

"Okay... Well, I was created over two thousand years ago and have lived in the Angelic Realm for most of that time. There were a few decades in the nineteen hundreds that I spent here on Earth. My favorite was the forties. That's when I met my friend, Grave..." He waved a hand through the air, "but that's a story for another time. There are different...levels of angels. I'm considered a Level Seven, which means my main focus is helping people who have fallen on hard times."

He stopped as Shane, eyes wide, poured another glass, taking a small sip.

"Are you okay?" Dax asked.

"Did... Did you just tell me that you're over two thousand years old?"

Dax swallowed. "Um... Yes?"

"Is that a question?"

"No." He laughed softly. "I just have never told anyone how old I am before."

"Never?"

He shrugged. "I've never had to."

"Oh." Shane took another sip of his drink. "And you live in a different realm?"

"Right now, yes. But I can live anywhere."

"And you help, like, natural disaster victims? People like that?"

"Not exactly. Yes, I've helped out in those situations, but my area is more...society disasters. Like a town that is failing because of a greedy mayor, or people who are in jeopardy of losing their homes because of a mortgage scam. Things like that. The major disasters...fires, earthquakes, tornadoes, et cetera...are more of a Level Ten issue. But, like I said, I've helped with those."

"Do you save people?"

"I try to." Dax paused as memories of people he was unable to save flashed through his mind. The type of disasters he dealt with may not be big in the grand scheme of things, but to a small group of individuals, it was all-encompassing. Sometimes the loss, pain, guilt, and self-loathing were too much for them to handle. He shrugged slightly. "I do what I can."

"You can't save everyone," Shane said softly, reaching out to briefly touch his arm before pulling back. "I'm sure you do wonderful work."

"Thank you."

"So, um... What exactly is an amans? I know you said it's something like a soulmate..."

"Exactly. You are the other half to my soul. Every being has one. Has that perfect someone who will complete them, love them for who they are and never leave their side. That's what we are. I knew it the second our eyes locked."

"Knew what?" Shane breathed.

"Knew you were important to me. Were going to be everything to me." Dax noticed a barrier start to descend over Shane's eyes. He had to convince him he would do anything for him. "If you commit to me, join your soul with mine, we will spend eternity together. You will have a life partner who will never leave you. Who will love you until the end of time."

Shane thought a moment. "That... That sounds wonderful, but nothing is ever just positive. There has to be a downside."

"Well..." Dax paused, then pushed on. "Like I said, we'll be together for eternity. Unfortunately, that means you'll have to pull away from the human world. If you don't, they'll notice you're not aging and start asking questions."

Tears welled in Shane's eyes as he whispered, "Jackson?"

"We'll tell him, of course, and I'll love and care for him as if he were my own. But, unless he also finds his soulmate in a paranormal, you'll eventually outlive him."

Shane was quiet, gazing out the window, taking everything in.

Dax knew he was probably overwhelmed with trying to take in so much information in a short amount of time. To find out your world was much different than you thought your whole life was definitely shocking. He hoped Shane wasn't going to push him away completely. The fear of the unknown sometimes made people act rashly.

"I think...," Shane said slowly, still looking out the window. Dax's heart squeezed at the uncertainty in his voice, not sure he wanted to hear the end of that sentence.

Dax glanced around the kitchen, waiting, knowing Shane would continue when he was ready. His gaze landed on several photos of Shane and Jackson, their smiling faces almost taunting him. He wanted that. Wanted a family. He'd been so excited about finding his amans, he never once thought he'd be rejected. What would he do? How would he be able to go on without him?

Hearing Shane release a soft sigh, Dax looked back at him, swallowing hard.

His eyes held a touch of sadness. Dax knew what was coming before he even opened his mouth, and he was powerless to stop it.

"I think I need some time," Shane said. "It's just... It's a lot to take in, Dax. And it's not just me I have to think about. What do I tell, Jackson? Do I tell him right now? It's all just..." He shook his head.

"A lot," Dax said softly, finishing his sentence. "I know it's a lot to take in, Shane. I just... Is there anything you need me to do to maybe explain this better?"

"I don't think so. I think this is something I just need to talk through in my head. Weigh the pros and cons." He gave him a slight smile and reached over, placing his hand on Dax's arm. "I appreciate you saving me. More than you know. While I don't completely understand it, I do sense there is something special between us. But..."

"But you need time." Dax smiled, though he knew it didn't reach his eyes. While he did understand where Shane was coming from...hell, he'd probably feel the same if the roles were reversed...he feared that if he were to walk away now, any progress he'd made would be lost. "Hopefully not too much time."

Shane snorted softly. "I really don't know. All I do know is I think time apart right now will be good."

Dax looked down at the hand still on his arm, committing the feeling of it to memory. While he truly hoped Shane wouldn't make him stay away for long, his heart told him to hold onto this moment. Just in case.

While he knew it would be hard, he'd walk away and give him the space he desired. Even though the thought almost broke him.

Chapter 9

Shane's Wish

"Shh... I got you."

Shane felt Dax's hand slide under his shirt, his rough fingers brushing against his flesh. He shivered from the contact, his body arching into the man's touch.

Tilting his head up, he licked Dax's lips, silently begging for more. With a roll of his hips, Dax had Shane panting, moaning as he frantically tried to get his jeans open.

"Slow down." His breath caressed Shane's cheek. "We're not in a hurry, are we?" Dax took his mouth in another scorching kiss.

Shane reveled in the feeling of his strong, hard body completely covering his. He craved this man, wondering how he'd lived his life without him.

"Dax," he gasped, ripping his mouth away. He felt Dax's heat as he dug his blunt fingernails into his sides. Then he gripped Shane's shirt and slowly pulled it over his head, dropping it to the floor.

"Look at you," Dax said as he began to make his way down Shane's chest, leaving a trail of hot kisses as he went. "I could just eat you up."

"Yes..." Shane threw his head back as Dax reached the top of his jeans, teasing the edge.

"If only you wanted me."

"W-what?" Shane spluttered and glanced down to find Dax looking at him, wings spread out.

"We could be doing this every day, if only you wanted me." Dax's green eyes seemed to take on a soft glow in the shadow now encompassing his face.

"I do want you." Shane reached for him, but Dax seemed to get farther away, just out of reach.

"No, my amans, you don't. It's time to wake up, love."

"But–"

"Wake up."

Wish a gasp, Shane sat up in bed, blinking furiously. It took him a minute to recognize his room. Falling back onto his pillow, chest heaving, he reached up and wiped the sweat off his face.

Shane shook his head. He'd never had a dream that vivid, that all-consuming. As much as it made him yearn for more, it also hurt his heart.

After Shane told him he needed time, Dax had called Grave to pick him up, telling him he'd explain about the car later. It was painful watching him leave, even if it was the right thing for him.

There was just so much to think about. So much he needed to mull over. Especially the fact the world he'd grown up in wasn't what he'd been taught.

An angel... Dax is an angel!

That thought had repeated in his head all afternoon, even after Cassie had brought Jackson home. She'd asked him how his date had gone, but the only word that came to mind was unexpected. Unexpected? That was the understatement of a century, but what could he say?

"It was going great until we got into a car accident, but Dax used his angel powers to get us out before we got hurt. Oh, I never mentioned Dax was an angel? It's okay, though, because I'm his soulmate."

Yeah, Shane could see that going over really well. So, instead, he chose to just smile and say he had a good time. He wasn't really lying. He did have a good time. Everything had been perfect, right up until the accident. After that, Shane felt like he fell through a wormhole or something. His heart knew every improbable thing that had taken place, every word that had left Dax's lips, was genuine...and he just didn't know what to do with that.

It wasn't so much the shock of finding out humans weren't the only beings that nagged at him. That was something he could deal with. No. It was the idea of Dax being his soulmate that had him breaking out into a cold sweat. There was no question he wanted Dax, but did he want to commit himself to somebody for all eternity?

On the other hand, would it really be so horrible? Sure, they didn't really know each other, but they had forever to learn all there was to know. Then there was the fact he wouldn't have to worry about losing him, which was an attractive idea. Shane didn't know if he could go through the pain of that again. But Jackson...

What if Jackson didn't find his soulmate? He'd eventually lose him, too.

Shane sucked in a breath, realizing that was the real reason he hesitated. How could he watch his little boy grow up, get old, and die?

Could he walk away from Dax, though? It had only been a few days, yet he already felt empty without him by his side.

These thoughts followed him through his morning routine. Getting dressed, making coffee, cooking breakfast...

While Shane leaned back against the counter, drinking his coffee, Jackson sat at the kitchen table, eating his pancakes, legs swinging slightly beneath the chair. It wasn't until he was almost done that his son finally looked up at him.

"What's wrong, Daddy? You have a funny look on your face."

"I just have a lot on my mind, kiddo. Nothing for you to worry about."

"Is it about Dax?"

Shane smiled slightly. This kid is too smart for his own good.

Walking over to the table, coffee in hand, Shane took a seat next to his son and watched him finish off the last of his breakfast. “Yes, it is.”

“What’s wrong? Don’t you like him?”

“I do like him. He’s very nice and fun to be around.”

“Then why do you look upset?”

“Because I don’t know if I should see him again.”

Jackson frowned and set his fork down before placing his hands in his lap. “But if you like him, why wouldn’t you want to see him?”

“Liking someone doesn’t mean they’re good for you.” At the confusion on Jackson’s face, Shane smiled and ran a hand through his son’s hair. “It’ll make sense when you’re older.”

“I like Dax, too. Can I still see him even if you don’t?”

“I... I don’t think it’ll work out that way, son.” When Jackson’s face fell, Shane felt his heart constrict. “Look. I’m still thinking everything over. So I don’t want you to worry about anything right now. Okay?”

"Okay, Daddy," Jackson said, voice still holding onto a hint of dejection.

He slid off the chair and carried his plate over to the sink, placing it onto the counter and pushing it back to ensure it wouldn't fall off.

"Daddy?" he said softly, not turning.

"Yeah, baby?"

After a moment, he turned to look at Shane. "I think you should keep Dax around."

He smiled at the look of concentration on his son's face. "You do, do you? And why do you think that?"

"Because you smile when you talk about him. If he makes you smile when he's not here, wouldn't it make you happier if he is?" Jackson shrugged, as if it were that simple, then headed up the stairs to his room.

Dax did make him happy. Happier than he'd been in a long, long time. If Shane did agree to this, they had years to spend with Jackson. Years to build memories and, hopefully, help him find his soulmate.

All of these thoughts ran through his head as the day went on. While he and Jackson made cookies that afternoon, joking and laughing, he had to force those thoughts out of his head several times. Luckily, Jackson didn't seem to notice, sneaking bites of raw cookie dough when he didn't think Shane was looking.

As he tucked Jackson into bed that night, Shane realized he'd finally made a decision. He did want Dax to be there. Wanted to include the man in their future, have him share in the memories.

"Daddy?"

"Hmm?" he hummed, tucking the comforter around his boy.

"Will you read me a story?"

"Of course, kiddo." Walking over to his son's bookcase, Shane's gaze landed on the book he'd read Jackson the other night. The one that caused his son to wish for his happiness. "Here we go," he said softly, pulling it off the shelf and sitting on the side of the bed.

The smile on his son's face brought a grin to his own as he opened the book and began to read. When he got to the part about wishing upon the Christmas Star, he paused, his mind drifting to Dax's sudden appearance on his lawn the morning after he'd heard his son make his wish.

Could that be it? Could Jackson's wish have brought Dax to them?

If he had thought that question just last week, he would have immediately laughed it off, called it ridiculous. Now, though, after all he'd seen, everything Dax had told him, Shane couldn't deny the possibility.

Hearing his son yawn, he shot him a gentle smile before continuing the story. By the time he was finished, Jackson was sound asleep. Shane stared at him for a bit, marveling in how much love he felt for his son, then returned the book to its shelf.

Turning off the lights, he glanced over at a soft glow in the corner. It was the miniature Christmas tree he'd bought Jackson on his first Christmas. That first year, he'd hung a small strand of multi-colored lights. Each year after that, he bought his son a new mini ornament for his tree. He'd put this year's ornament, a kitten wearing a Santa hat, into his stocking, along with some other goodies.

Shane made his way to his room and gathered all of Jackson's presents. He couldn't afford to get him a lot, but he truly hoped the toys and clothes he bought would bring a smile to his son's face. Between what he made from his editing service and David's life insurance, he was able to take care of their bills and buy food, with little money left over for anything else.

He tapped one of his apps on his phone, starting some Christmas music as he readied the front room for the morning, anxious to see the wonder in his son's eyes when he woke up.

It didn't take him long before he was done and stood back, looking around. Shane smiled. Everything looked perfect, right down to the plate of cookies for Santa Jackson had set out before going to bed.

He stretched his arms above his head, his back giving a plethora of crackles and pops. He turned off the lights and began to make his way up the stairs, yawning several times as he walked into his room. His gaze strayed to David's side of the bed, like it had every night for the last five years. But it seemed different now. Before, he'd curl up with David's pillow and cry himself to sleep. But now he just felt sad. Sad David wasn't around to see Jackson grow up.

It wasn't until that moment, staring at the bed they once shared, that he realized something. Dax wouldn't replace David. In fact, Shane had a feeling he'd want to hear everything they shared in their time together. Would encourage him to talk about him.

David is probably up in heaven yelling at me right now. Telling me to stop overthinking everything. That I deserve to be happy again, Shane thought with a shake of his head.

Turning off the light, he glanced at his bedroom window. The moon outside filtered through the blinds, giving the room a soft, inviting glow. It called to him. What he contemplated seemed crazy, but if it worked for Jackson, maybe it would work for him.

Walking to the window, Shane pulled up the blinds to reveal the back yard, trees lining the fence. The blanket of snow seemed to sparkle in the moonlight.

He looked up at the moon, its brilliance demanding attention. The only thing that rivaled it was the Christmas Star.

Could it be that easy? Shane asked himself. Leaning against the windowsill, he pushed away the slight feeling of absurdity and blew out a soft breath.

"I feel like I should recite some poetry or something. Then again, I'd probably feel even more ridiculous than I do now."

He ran a hand through his short hair, giving it a little tug as he tried to organize his thoughts.

"Okay... So I'm not sure how this works, but I want to start by thanking you for sending Dax to me. He has only been in our life a short time, but I already feel like I can't imagine our future without him. But a part of me is still unsure. I'm so worried it's a mistake to bond with him. That I'll just end up getting hurt. Then again, what if I push him away and miss out on something wonderful? I guess..." Shane blew out another breath. "I guess what I really need is a sign on what I should do."

He looked out over the back yard again, at the crisp snow and dark purple shadows cast by the surrounding trees. It was beautiful, magical, and made this seem like a fairytale. His gaze traveled back up to the bright star, heart clenching as he tried to put his fears and hopes into a single wish.

"I wish... I wish I was certain about what to do, that what my heart wants is the right thing. Not just for myself, but for Jackson. He would be heartbroken if Dax isn't the man he thinks he is. That I think he is."

Shane stood there a moment longer before closing the blinds and sliding into bed. He curled on his side, staring at the pillow beside him, and felt a longing to not be alone. Images of Dax lying next to him, smiling at him, flashed into his mind as he slowly began to drift off.

Chapter 10

What's An Angel To Do?

"Would you stop pacing and moaning? You're giving me anxiety."

Dax stopped and turned to glare at Grave. "I'm not moaning. I'm just trying to figure out what to do."

"Well, he said he needed time to figure everything out, so that's what you need to give him."

"I am, but I still feel like I should do...something. Maybe get him and Jackson something for Christmas. Not just sit around and stare at you for..." He waved his hand around," however long."

"You could always give him a call or text him. You guys did exchange numbers before you left yesterday. So that must mean he's okay with you calling him."

"We exchanged numbers because I told him to call me when he's ready. Not so I could bombard his phone with messages and..." Dax threw his hands into the air, "and smiley or kissy faces. Plus, wouldn't that go against his need for space anyway?"

"You're right. Maybe stepping back is the best thing you can do for him right now. What better gift to give someone than time? I think there's even a song or two about that."

"Really?!"

"Hey. No need to get your feathers ruffled." He chuckled as Dax glared and did just that with his wings. "I'm just saying he asked for time, so the best thing you can do is give that to him."

Grave picked up another slice of pizza they'd ordered for dinner. Dax watched as the light in the room seemed to reflect off his friend's silver eyes, making them almost shimmer. His short, black-and-green-streaked hair stood on end, as if he'd repeatedly run his hands through it. The black color was natural. The green the one he'd chosen for today. Grave told him he wanted to be festive. Dax had to admit, it looked good on him. Added color that contrasted with his black shirt and pants and dark skin.

"If you want to do something for him and his son for Christmas, I'm sure they'd like it. But as a friend. Don't go crazy and push things."

Dax once again began to move around the front room of the house they were currently renting. Airbnb's had become a real convenience for those paranormals who moved around a lot. It gave them a nice place to stay and, for the most part, the owners didn't ask any questions. This house was a cozy two-bedroom ranch with a small, fenced-in back yard. At the moment, though, all Dax could concentrate on was the fact Shane was a mere five blocks away. Not that distance really mattered to a paranormal, but knowing he was close made him feel a little better.

"Okay... I'll do something for them for Christmas..." He stopped pacing, letting out a low growl, "which is tomorrow. Dammit. What should I do?"

"I don't know," Grave mumbled around a mouthful of pizza. His friend looked around the room, as if the answer to his question was in there with them. His gaze settled on their dinner. "How about pizza? Everyone likes pizza."

Dax rolled his eyes. "Grave, I am not getting them pizza for Christmas. Be serious. It needs to be something special."

"Special, huh?" He swallowed the last bite of his pizza and studied Dax. "I mean, I know he's your amans, but you don't really know the man yet."

"I know, but it has to have meaning."

"Hmm..."

Grave tapped his fingers against his leg, brows scrunched in concentration. He had always been a good friend. They'd been through a lot together. While most wouldn't think an angel and a demon could get along, he'd always trusted Grave above everyone else, and vice versa. For that reason, he hoped his friend would be able to think of something perfect.

"What about a puppy?"

Or maybe not, Dax thought.

"I don't think that's a good idea. At least not without clearing it with Shane first."

At Grave's nod, Dax walked over to the window and looked out over the snow-covered lawn. The full moon shone down, causing the snow to give off a bluish sparkle. It was stunning. Was Shane looking upon the same scene from his bedroom window? Would they ever be able to share this sight? If only he could get Shane to trust him enough to take a leap of faith.

He knew his hesitation stemmed from the loss of his partner. While Dax had never known pain like that, he did understand Shane's need to protect his heart. If only there were a way to get him to see that he wasn't trying to take his husband's place. That it was okay to continue living and find love. Dax was sure his husband would have wanted that.

Then an idea came to him. It started as a passing thought, but as he slowly turned to look at Grave, a small smile on his face, the idea began to take root.

"I know what to do."

Dax started pacing again, talking to himself. "I must find him, see if this is something he can help me with. If he can... This is going to be perfect."

Grave jumped up and grabbed his arm, stopping him, eyes narrowed. "Hold up. What are you talking about?"

His smile widened as he stared at his friend. "The perfect gift for Shane. Something special. Something only I can give him."

"What's that?"

"A chance," Dax said softly. "A chance to say goodbye."

Chapter 11

Finding The Right Words

Shane looked at the snow-covered bushes, lights twinkling. Turning slowly, he spotted a statue not far from him, a bench right beneath it. The bench was new, but he definitely recognized everything else. He was in The Garden, yet didn't feel the cold.

"A dream...," he whispered.

Walking toward the bench, Shane wondered if there were a reason for this. He'd never had a dream before where he actually knew he was dreaming.

"It's so quiet," he mused, voice echoing slightly around him. He glanced down, realizing that he couldn't hear the snow crunching beneath his feet. "Why am I here?"

"You've always liked it here."

Shane's heart stuttered and breath caught as he stumbled to a stop, but he didn't turn around to face the owner of that voice. One he'd know anywhere. Fear kept him from moving. Not fear of seeing someone behind him, but fear that he wouldn't.

"Shane, please, turn around."

Taking a shaky breath, Shane slowly turned. Even though he knew who'd be standing there, it still didn't prepare him for the shock.

David...

His blond hair was messy, just like it used to be when he rolled out of bed. His bright, blue eyes, eyes Shane remembered getting lost in, gazed at him warmly. He looked good, just like he did that fateful morning before he left for work. The last time Shane had seen him alive.

"David?" Shane whispered, tears rolling down his cheeks. "I don't understand."

"Oh, Shane," he said, taking a few steps toward him, a smile on his face. "Look at you. As handsome as ever. Even in your pajamas."

Shane glanced down. He didn't even realize he was wearing his pajamas, which contained cartoon Santas and flying reindeer. "Jackson picked these out for me," he said absently, tugging at the bottom of his shirt. Looking back up, he gave David a small smile as his eyes took in everything about the man before him. From his well-worn, blue, button-down shirt, to David's fitted, dark blue jeans and black boots. "You look good, too."

"Thanks. It would seem that when you die, you stay in whatever clothes you had on when you passed." David smiled. "Good thing it was a casual Friday at work, huh?"

Shane let out a sob as he launched himself forward and wrapped his arms around David. The feeling of being pulled into an embrace he had missed so much was his undoing. His body shuddered as soul-wrenching cries burst from his lips.

All of the pain he'd buried broke free, and he was helpless to stop it.

"I am so sorry," David whispered against the top of Shane's head.

Pulling back, tears streaming down his face, Shane looked into David's eyes. The blue of them was a little brighter than he remembered. Another soft sob left his lips as David reached up and cupped his face, his thumb gently wiping away his tears.

“I’ve missed you so much,” Shane choked out.

“I’ve missed you, too, but I’ve never truly left. I’ve always been here, watching you, loving you. You have done so well with Jackson. He is such an amazing little boy. I couldn’t be prouder of both of you.”

“He’s the only thing that keeps me from falling apart.”

“That may be true, but I know how strong you are, even when you think you’re weak. I had faith you’d be okay, even without Jackson.” David placed a soft kiss on Shane’s forehead, lingering for a moment before pulling back. “I wish I could have come to you sooner.”

Shane’s brows furrowed. “How are you here?”

“I really shouldn’t be, but a rather...persuasive angel convinced the higher-ups this was something we both needed.”

Images of Dax came to mind, making Shane smile. “He wouldn’t happen to have green eyes and red hair, would he?”

“And a killer smile and hot body.” David chuckled. “You wouldn’t happen to know him, would you?”

“Just a bit.” Shane’s smile slowly slipped. “He says we’re soulmates.”

David grinned. “I didn’t know there was anything other than humans when I was alive, but after...” He shrugged. “Let’s just say my eyes got opened really quickly to the fact we’re not alone. I have heard about their soulmates. If this angel says you are his soulmate, then you are. It’s not something any of them take lightly. I’m happy for you, too.”

“You are?”

“Yes. The last thing I want is for you to live the rest of your life alone. You are an amazing man. Somebody else needs to experience that.”

“I won’t be alone. I have Jackson.”

David frowned. “You know what I mean, Shane. I’d feel a lot better knowing you have someone to watch over you. Someone to love you and feel your love in return.”

Shane felt his eyes start to well with tears again, so he blew out a breath and tried to rein in his emotions. He knew this would be the only time he’d ever get to say goodbye to his first love. The last thing he wanted was cry the whole time.

“I don’t know...”

He'd always love David. Was that fair to Dax? Did he have room in his heart to love both?

While his mind might still be struggling, his heart wasn't.

"Love him, Shane. Allow him to be a part of your life." David pulled him in for a tight hug, squeezing him. "I just want you to be happy, to live life. What you've been doing since I died is not living. You've just been existing. Moving forward with your life, opening yourself up to love again, will never change the way we felt about each other, never overshadow what we had."

Leaning back, David looked at him, gaze full of love and understanding. "Tell me you're going to give him a chance. That you're going to move forward with your life and be happy."

Shane nodded. "I will. I love you so much, David. I always will."

"And do this for you. Not just because I asked you to. Okay?"

"Okay."

"Okay," he said softly. "I've got to go."

"No." Shane's voice caught as he tried to hold onto David's arms.

He placed a finger against his lips. “Shh... Everything is going to be okay. I promise.” David stepped back, placing one of his hands on Shane’s chest. “Just remember, even though you can’t see me, I’ll always be with you. Always love you.”

“I love you.” Shane wrapped his arms around himself. “And I miss you so much.”

“I love and miss you, too. But it’s okay to say goodbye.”

“I’m not ready,” Shane uttered.

“I know, but you need to.”

Gazing into David’s eyes one last time, Shane tried to memorize everything about him. He wanted to imprint this moment onto his very soul. Even though he wasn’t ready to say goodbye, probably never would be, he also knew it was time.

“Close your eyes,” David whispered.

Taking one last look, Shane slowly closed his eyes. He stood there silently, jumping slightly when he felt a light brush of lips against his. A kiss that promised everlasting love. David lingered for a moment before Shane felt his warmth pull away, knowing that was his way of saying goodbye.

Shane stood there, not wanting to open his eyes to confirm he was alone. He felt a softness at his back, a cushiness beneath his head.

Opening his eyes, Shane found himself back in his bedroom, moonlight streaming through the window, tears trickling down his cheeks. He glanced at the clock on his nightstand. Almost five in the morning

Jackson would probably wake up at any time now, excited to see what Santa had left him. Shane rubbed his hands down his face, eyes burning. Yet he felt better than he had in a long time. Like a weight had been lifted.

Taking a fortifying breath, he looked over at David's side of the bed. He almost saw him lying there, one arm under his head as he gazed at him, grin on his face. Shane smiled as the image slowly faded, leaving a warmth in his chest.

Grabbing his phone from the nightstand, he sent off a quick text, which was immediately answered. Smiling, he looked up at the ceiling.

"Goodbye, David," he whispered. "Love you."

As he swung his legs over the bed and stood, he heard the sound of little feet heading his way.

"Daddy!" Jackson yelled as he burst into the room, body filled with the kind of excitement only a Christmas morning caused. An excitement that, for the first holiday in years, he felt echoing in his soul.

Chapter 12

All I Want For Christmas

Dax stood on the doorstep, nervous, yet excited. To say he'd been surprised to receive Shane's text message was putting it mildly. It was just a simple text, Shane inviting him over for Christmas, but it meant so much. Especially since he wasn't sure how his gift was received.

It had taken a bit of persuading to convince the higher-ups to allow David to visit Shane. Dax had almost lost the argument at one point. They had very strict rules about visiting loved ones from the afterlife. But after explaining how Shane was his amans and needed closure to move on, they had given in, albeit begrudgingly.

Now Dax stood there, unsure of what to say. Should he bring up what he'd done? Wait to see if Shane brought it up? Maybe not say anything at all?

“This is crazy. Just man up and knock on the door,” he mumbled, rolling his shoulders, the bag of presents in his hand crinkling softly. “You were invited, for fuck’s sake.”

Dax took a deep breath and knocked. The sound of running on the other side soon reached his ears. A smile spread across his face as the door opened to reveal a bright-eyed Jackson staring up at him.

“Dax!” he squealed, bouncing. “You’re here!”

“I am. Merry Christmas.”

“Merry Christmas,” the boy giggled.

“Jackson, I thought I told you to not open the door without me.”

Hearing the voice, Dax’s whole body warmed. Shane walked around the corner, their gazes locking.

“Hey,” Shane said softly, cheeks reddening.

“Hey.” Dax licked his lips, just barely repressing the urge to lunge forward and pull the man into an earth-shattering kiss. “Oh... Here.” He held out the bag of presents. “Merry Christmas.”

"You didn't have to get us–" Shane started.

"More presents!" Jackson exclaimed, taking the bag and rushing toward the living room. "Thanks, Dax!"

Shane chuckled. "Well... Thank you for the gifts, and for coming over."

"Since I wanted to see you, there was no way I was going to say no."

"I wanted to see you, too."

"Yeah?"

"Yeah. Want a cup of coffee? I just poured myself one."

"I would love one." Dax stepped close, closing the door behind him. "But first..."

"Yes?" Shane swallowed.

Dax leaned down to capture Shane's lips. Feeling his body melt into his arms made Dax feel like he'd just come home. Like this was where he needed to be.

Gradually ending the kiss, knowing Jackson might come around the corner any minute and he wasn't ready to explain what they both meant to him, Dax nipped Shane's bottom lip before straightening. The look of pure bliss on Shane's face made him want to push his chest out in pride.

"Come on! I want to open my presents!" Jackson yelled from the living room.

Shane cleared his throat. "We'll be right there!" He looked back up at Dax. "Why don't you go sit with Jackson and I'll bring out the coffee?"

"Sounds good."

Dax walked to where Jackson bounced on the couch. "Hi, little man."

"I'm not little," Jackson laughed. "You're just really tall."

"That I am." Dax chuckled, glancing around the room.

The tree was beautiful in its simplicity. Hand-painted baubles and store-bought ornaments were spread out perfectly, multi-colored lights wrapped around it. A gorgeous angel, illuminated from the inside by a single, white light, rested at the very top. A few presents sat beneath the tree.

Once Shane walked in, handing him his coffee and sitting next to him on the couch, Jackson attacked the gifts. Watching the young boy open each with so much enthusiasm made Dax's smile widen.

He wanted this to be his family. His life.

As Jackson opened the last of the presents from his father and Santa...which consisted of clothes, books, and toys...it was time to open the gifts Dax had brought.

"Here. Let me," he said, setting his coffee onto the table and pulling over the bag he'd brought. Reaching in, he pulled out a box, Jackson's name scrawled across the top. "This one's for you."

Jackson walked on his knees over to him and reached for the box, hugging it to his chest with a huge smile.

"What do you say, Jackson?" Shane asked.

"Sorry," the boy said, turning to Dax. "Thank you."

"You're welcome."

"Sorry. He just gets so excited." Shane glanced at him before looking back at his son, watching him rip through the wrapping paper.

“It’s Christmas. He should be excited.” Dax reached over and wrapped his arm around Shane’s shoulders, pulling him close. Shane stiffened for a moment, glancing between him and Jackson several times before relaxing.

“Oh, wow,” Jackson breathed as he pulled something out of the box.

“What is it, buddy?” Shane asked.

“Dad…” Jackson stood, walking toward the couch. “Look what Dax got me.”

When he’d been trying to figure out what to get him, an image of a bright star suddenly came to Dax’s mind. So he pulled his magic together and created what he thought would be the perfect star. It wasn’t anything special, but the look of wonder on Jackson’s face told him differently.

It wasn’t large, maybe about two feet by three feet. The cuts he’d put in the crystal made up the star, and he’d gotten other angels to fill it with blue, green, yellow, and pink hues. More than that, though, Dax had left a bit of his own magic in the center of it, making it shimmer with its own light.

“How pretty,” Shane said, taking it from Jackson’s outstretched hand. “It even has a silver ribbon at the top so you can hang it on your wall, or maybe in the window so it can catch the sunlight."

"I actually have an ornament stand in the car, so if he wants, he can place it on his desk or dresser."

"That would be great."

"Thank you, Dax. You got me my Christmas Star."

Dax wasn't sure about that, but if Jackson wanted it to be his Christmas Star, that was what it would be.

Grabbing the other box in his bag, Dax turned to Shane and handed him his present. "I hope you like it."

"I'm sure I will." Shane smiled as he slowly removed the wrapping paper, setting it next to him before pulling off the lid.

Dax felt nervous, second-guessing himself. Sure, the image had suddenly come to mind, just like the one for the star. But that didn't mean Shane would like it.

"Oh, Dax," he said softly, pulling the gift from the box. The round ornament gleamed as Shane held it by its ribbon, watching it spin slightly.

The soft colors painted across the smooth surface made up a beautiful picture that Dax had created from memory. One of him and Shane standing in The Garden, surrounded by snow, white lights seeming to twinkle, the statue behind them. That moment was forever etched in his mind. The moment he realized how much he loved the man standing next to him.

"How did you...," Shane began, voice cracking as he ran his thumb over the picture.

"Daddy, are you okay?"

He quickly wiped a stray tear from his cheek. "Yeah, kiddo. I'm fine. Just really happy."

"I'm glad you like it." Dax smiled, watching Shane hold the ornament reverently.

"I love it. It's perfect."

Reaching into the bag, Dax pulled out a baggy containing an ornament hook. "Do you want to hang it?"

Shane took the hook from him and walked up to the tree. He stood there for a moment, seemingly looking for the perfect branch. Jackson got up, too, standing beside his dad, both studying the tree.

"What do you think?" Shane asked, looking down at his son.

"Hmm... I think you should put it there." He pointed to a branch just a little above his head.

Shane cleared his throat. The sudden rush of emotions he felt radiating off his amans made Dax stand and walk up to him. While he definitely exuded happiness and love, there was also an underlying sadness.

Deciding to throw caution to the wind, Dax wrapped his arms around Shane, pulling him back into his chest. "Are you okay?" he asked softly.

"I am. It's just..." He sighed and nodded at an ornament right next to where Jackson indicated. "That's the last ornament David gave me."

Dax tightened his arms around him, remaining silent. After a few moments, Shane leaned forward and gently placed the new ornament on the branch to the right, hanging it just slightly lower than the other one.

"Perfect," Shane murmured.

"It really is." Dax placed a kiss on the top of his head.

He patted Dax's arm around his middle. "David would have liked you, you know."

"Really?"

"Yeah. I know he's happy you are here with us."

Felling a little hand on his hip, he glanced down to see Jackson grasping his shirt, looking up at the ornaments. The moment felt perfect.

"This is going to be great. You'll see, Shane. I love you."

Dax leaned back slightly as Shane turned in his arms. The warmth and love in his eyes almost brought him to his knees.

"Are we going to be a family?" Jackson asked softly, looking up at them.

"Yes," Shane said, smiling at Jackson. "We sure are."

"And you're going to make my daddy happy, Dax?"

Releasing one arm from around Shane, he reached down and scooped up Jackson, holding him against his side as he met his gaze. "I'm going to make your daddy and you very happy for the rest of our lives. I promise."

Jackson was silent a moment, his eyes searching Dax's. Then and dove at him, wrapping his slim arms around Dax's neck. "I knew my wish would come true."

Dax glanced at Shane, confused. But the smile on his face and single tear running down his cheek prevented him from asking any questions. Finding out what Jackson meant didn't matter, as long as both were content.

Jackson pulled back and smiled. "Merry Christmas, Daddy. Merry Christmas, Dax."

"Merry Christmas, kiddo," Shane said, leaning in and hugging Jackson. Glancing over his son's head, Shane met Dax's eyes. The look in them promised a life filled with love and wonder.

This was his family. What he'd waited for his entire life. Sure, there was more they needed to discuss, especially about revealing to Jackson who he was. But there would be time for that later. For now, this moment... Everything was perfect.

"Merry Christmas," Dax said, leaning in to give Shane a soft kiss before hugging them both tightly. Looking at the tree, his gaze landed on the ornament David had given Shane. It sparkled with a soft glow, giving off a warmth that touched his very soul. He was thankful for whatever David had said to Shane in his dream, vowing to find the man one day and thank him properly.

He'd always loved the holiday, marveled at the magic and beauty of it. This Christmas, though, would definitely stay with him for eternity.

"Merry Christmas, Dax. I love you," he heard Shane say, his fingers tightening on his back.

They were safe in each other's arms, filling the air around them with love and happiness.

This moment was perfection. It was everything. It was family.

And that was the best gift ever.

Smiling, Chiara placed the mirrored snowflake on the shelf, next to all the other Christmas wishes she'd granted over the years. Each snowflake was unique, beautiful, and filled her heart with joy.

Jackson's wish had been especially moving to her. The innocence of it, the purity of his reasons touched her soul. So it had been a pleasure to make his wish come true. Not to mention the excitement of watching Dax and Shane come together. Chiara knew it wasn't going to be an immediate fix for the man's soul, but she had faith in the angel's ability to see what Shane really needed.

She was still amazed Dax had the guts to ask the higher-ups for David to visit Shane and give him that much-needed closure. It was brilliant. Even Chiara hadn't seen that coming.

"And how did your Christmas season go, Sister?"

Turning, Chiara smiled at her brother, Drystan. "It went well, actually. Really well."

"Yeah?" He made his way over to her well-worn couch and sank into it with a sigh, chuckling. "Judging from the look in your eyes, I'd say you've been up to some mischief."

Laughing, she walked over and sat next to him, shifting so she could look at him. They were siblings in name only. They were created on the same day, but had different jobs. While she was a Christmas Spirit, Drystan was an Emotional Spirit. He managed the needs and wishes of those in the most dire of circumstances. She didn't know how he handled the humans' pain and suffering, understanding she wouldn't be strong enough for that job. He often came to her and asked how her job was going. Probably for the levity of her work more than anything. A little light in his darkness.

"Not mischief so much," she responded. "More like...matchmaking."

"Oh? And what was the wish that brought this on?"

Chiara gazed into her brother's deep blue eyes. So different than her forest green ones. "A little boy who wished his daddy wasn't so sad and lonely anymore. You know how I am when it comes to the pure and innocent." At Drystan's knowing grin, Chiara shrugged. "Plus, it turns out his dad is the soulmate of our very own Dax?"

Her brother's eyes widened. "The angel?"

"The one and only."

He whistled softly. "How did that go over?"

"Just as you would expect." Chiara smiled. "Beautifully."

"So you granted a child his Christmas wish and brought a fated pair together all in one shot?" Drystan asked, sounding impressed.

She shrugged playfully. "What can I say? I'm good at my job. With just the right nudge, things have a way of working themselves out."

"That they do."

"What about you? How was your last case?"

A sad look crossed his face momentarily before he blinked and smiled once again. "Let's not talk about me and my troubles right now. It's Christmas. I want to spend it with my favorite sister, listening to how you managed to get Dax to settle down."

Deciding to let it go, for now, Chiara leaned back and got comfortable. "It all started with me yanking Dax from his home and depositing him on Shane's lawn."

Drystan stared at her, then burst out laughing. "Chiara, you didn't..."

"I most certainly did. Then it got really fun."

Thank You

Thank you for picking up a copy of my Christmas novella. This was a labor of love, and I truly enjoyed writing Dax and Shane's story.

I want to say thank you to my family and friends for answering my silly questions and helping me give my characters a voice.

Thank you to my editor for your hard work and dedication, helping me tell their story the way they wanted before all my words got in the way.

A huge thank you to the members of my fan group for inspiring and supporting me. Also, for helping me decide on a title. You guys are the best.

And a special thank you to Lisa K. for helping me come up with Jackson's name. I was having a tough time coming up with one. When you commented with the name Jackson, I knew it was perfect.

I hope you all enjoyed my book. Please consider leaving a review. Your comments not only help my work be noticed, but also help me continue doing what I love.

Until next time, darlings... Take care of

yourselves, and each other.

From my family to yours, Merry Christmas!

E.F. Rose xx

About the Author

E.F. Rose and family have found their corner of the world in the Central Valley of California. She has always enjoyed writing and considers herself to be a multi-genre author, with urban fantasy and dark romance being her main focus. If she isn't writing up a storm, she can be found chatting with friends, reading a good book, or spending time with her husband and son.

If you would like to know more about E.F. Rose and her work, you can find all her social media and book links at https://linktr.ee/E_F_Rose, or you can reach out to her at emilyfrose13@gmail.com.

"You are my drive, my inspiration, the life behind my words."

More Work From E.F. Rose

Echoes (A Book of Poetry)

The Fallen Guardians Series

Divinely Entwined (Book 1) – Christian & Ella

Bound in Fate (Book 2) – Manuel & Hayley

Tangled in Tinsel (Book 2.5)

Faithfully Entangled (Book 3) – Nicholas & Amy

Twisted Mercy (Book 4) – Cyrus' Story *coming soon*

Wicked Rogues

Maverick Rising (Prequel) – Maverick & Jenny, part of the "Wrong Side of the Tracks" anthology

Forever Knight (Book 1) – Tristan & Abby

Always Abby (Book 2) – Tristan & Abby *coming soon*

Standalone Novellas

Colin's Valentine's Day Surprise – Colin & Brett

An Angel for Christmas – Shane & Dax

www.ingramcontent.com/pod-product-compliance
Lightning Source LLC
LaVergne TN
LVHW010625100826
845148LV00014B/3112

* 9 7 9 8 9 8 5 2 1 1 2 7 6 *